Lilly's Big Day

KEVIN HENKES

Greenwillow Books

An Imprint of HarperCollinsPublishers

For Clara

Lilly's Big Day

Copyright © 2006 by Kevin Henkes

All rights reserved. Manufactured in China.

www.harperchildrens.com

Watercolor paints and a black pen
were used to prepare the full-color art.
The text type is 16-point Mrs. Eaves Bold.

Library of Congress Cataloging-in-Publication Data
Lilly's big day / Kevin Henkes.
"Greenwillow Books."
 p. cm.
Summary: When her teacher announces that he is getting
married, Lilly the mouse sets her heart on being the flower
girl at his wedding.
ISBN-10: 0-06-074236-4 (trade bdg.) ISBN-13: 978-0-06-074236-2 (trade bdg.)
ISBN-10: 0-06-074237-2 (lib. bdg.) ISBN-13: 978-0-06-074237-9 (lib. bdg.)
[1. Mice—Fiction. 2. Weddings—Fiction.
3. Teachers—Fiction.] I. Title.
PZ7.H389Lg 2005 [E]—dc22 2004052263

First Edition 10 9 8 7 6 5 4 3 2 1

One day Lilly's teacher, Mr. Slinger, announced to the class
that he was going to marry Ms. Shotwell, the school nurse.
Lilly's heart leaped. She had always wanted to be a flower girl.
"It will be the biggest day of my life," said Mr. Slinger.
"Mine, too," whispered Lilly.

At home in her room, Lilly practiced being a flower girl.
First she changed into something more appropriate.
Then she held her head high
and smiled brightly
and raised her eyebrows
and turned her head from side to side
and carried her hands proudly in front of her
and hummed "Here Comes the Bride"
and walked the length of her room very, very slowly.
Back and forth, back and forth, back and forth.

"It will be the biggest day of my life," said Lilly.

"Who are you pretending to be tonight?"
  asked Lilly's mother at dinner.
"I'm not pretending," said Lilly. "I'm a flower girl."
"Who's getting married?" asked her father.
"Mr. Slinger," said Lilly.
"Really?" said her mother.
"Really?" said her father.

"Really," said Lilly. "He's going to marry Ms. Shotwell.
He told us today. And I'm going to be the flower girl."
"You are?" said her father.
"Did Mr. Slinger ask you?" said her mother.
"Not yet," said Lilly.

At bedtime Lilly's mother said, "Lilly, there are so many students in your class. Mr. Slinger couldn't possibly pick just one to be a flower girl."

Her father said, "It wouldn't be fair."

"He probably has a niece . . . ," said her mother.

"Maybe Aunt Mona will get married someday . . . ," said her father.

"Do you understand what we're trying to say?" asked her mother.

Lilly nodded.

"Are you sure?" asked her father.

Lilly nodded again.

After her parents left her room, Lilly said, "I understand that I'm going to be a flower girl."

The next day at school during Sharing Time, Lilly said, "I've always wanted to be a flower girl. Even more than a surgeon or a diva or a hairdresser."

The following afternoon when Mr. Slinger had recess duty, Lilly picked a handful of weeds at the edge of the playground. She carried the weeds proudly in front of her and walked very, very slowly past Mr. Slinger until the bell rang. Back and forth, back and forth, back and forth.

And the morning after that, Lilly went to the Lightbulb Lab in the back of the classroom. She drew a self-portrait.

Mr. Slinger called Lilly up to his desk during Quiet Reading Time. "Lilly," he said, "I can tell that you want to be a flower girl, but unfortunately my niece, Ginger, is going to be the flower girl at my wedding."

Lilly's heart sank.

"But," said Mr. Slinger, "I also want you to know that everyone in the class will be invited to the wedding. We can all dance together at the reception. It'll be fun."

Lilly's stomach hurt.

"This seems really important to you," said Mr. Slinger.

Lilly's cheeks turned pink.

"You know . . . ," said Mr. Slinger, "I was just thinking that you might like to be Ginger's assistant. You could stand with her and keep her company until she has to walk down the aisle. You could make sure her dress isn't crooked and that she holds her flowers properly."

Lilly considered this.

"You could remind her to walk slowly," said Mr. Slinger.

Lilly considered some more.

"You could wear a corsage," said Mr. Slinger.

"Oh, all right," said Lilly, "if you really need me so much."

Lilly tried to get excited about being Ginger's assistant.

"Weddings wouldn't even exist without flower girl assistants," she told her baby brother, Julius.

"I have a special responsibility," she told her parents.

When her Grammy took her shopping for a new dress for the wedding, Lilly told the clerk, "A flower girl assistant is *very* important. Important *and* glamorous."

But when it really sank in that she would not be walking
down the aisle carrying a bouquet with everyone watching,
Lilly pretended that her teddy bear was Mr. Slinger.
She made him sit in the Uncooperative Chair.
"You can just stay there forever," she said.

As the wedding drew near, Mr. Slinger counted down the days on the chalkboard.

"One day closer to the biggest day of my life," he would say.

"One day closer to the biggest day of *Ginger's* life," Lilly would whisper.

And still, at home in her room, Lilly practiced.
  She held her head high
    and smiled brightly
      and raised her eyebrows
        and turned her head from side to side
          and carried her hands proudly in front of her
            and hummed "Here Comes the Bride"
              and walked the length of her room very, very slowly.
                Back and forth, back and forth, back and forth.

The day of the wedding finally arrived.
Lilly hoped and hoped that Ginger would have pinkeye
or a bad fever and not show up.
But she was there. And she was all ready. Her dress was
straight and she held her flowers properly.

"Are you sure you want to do this?" said Lilly.

"Yes," said Ginger.

"Are you sure you're sure?"

"Yes."

"Are you *really* sure you're sure?"

Lilly hoped and hoped that Ginger would change her mind.

But she didn't.

It was time for the ceremony to begin.

The music swelled.

Everyone stood.

The moment came for Ginger to walk down the aisle.

Ginger didn't move.

Mr. Slinger motioned her forward.

"Go," said Lilly.

Ginger was frozen.

"Now," said Lilly.

Ginger was as still as a stone.

"You can do it," said Lilly.

But Ginger couldn't.

Everyone waited. And waited. And waited.

No one knew what to do—except Lilly.

Lilly scooped up Ginger and said, "Here we go."

Then Lilly walked very, very slowly down the aisle.

She held her head high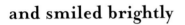

and smiled brightly

and raised her eyebrows

and turned her head from side to side

and carried Ginger proudly in front of her.

When she reached Mr. Slinger, everyone clapped.
"I knew this would be the biggest day of my life!" said Lilly.

Lilly was so excited she barely noticed the rest of the ceremony.

The reception was great fun.

After the cake was served, Lilly coached Ginger for the next time she would be a flower girl.

"I won't be with you at every wedding," said Lilly. "I won't be able to save you every time."

Together they walked back and forth,
back and forth,
back and forth,
very, very slowly.

Soon they were dancing.

And soon after that, they were joined by Chester, Wilson,
Victor, Julius, Mr. Slinger, Ms. Shotwell, and many others.
"It's Interpretive Dance!" said Mr. Slinger.
"We're doing the Flower Girl!" said Lilly.

Lilly's family stayed at the reception until Lilly was perfectly exhausted.

"But there's something I have to do before we go," said Lilly.

She needed to find Ginger one last time.

And when she did, she said, "Ginger, when I get married,
you can be my flower girl."